Bluebird Finds a Home

story by Ryan Jacobson and illustrations by Joel Seibel

Adventure Publications, Inc.
Cambridge, MN

Dedication

For Jonah and Lucas,
You make my world a better place.

—Ryan Jacobson

Nest box photo (pg. 29) by Stan Tekiela
Cover and book design by Jonathan Norberg
Edited by Brett Ortler

10 9 8 7 6 5 4 3 2 1

Published by Adventure Publications, Inc.
820 Cleveland St. S
Cambridge, MN 55008
1-800-678-7006
www.adventurepublications.net

Printed in China

ISBN-13: 978-1-59193-314-4
ISBN-10: 1-59193-314-5

Meet the Nature Squad

A rumble echoed through the woods.

"That sounds like thunder," said Mr. Rivers.

Not thunder. B.B. was hungry. The bear's stomach groaned as he scanned the clearing.

Workers cut down all the dead trees, thought the bear. *No big deal. At least they left plenty of garbage to eat.*

B.B. didn't see any food scraps though. Instead, he found his Nature Squad buddies picking up the litter.

Kingston fluttered onto a stump beside the bear. “Where have you been? I ordered everyone to help clean this mess.”

B.B. didn’t have a good excuse. He had been showing the workers even more dead trees to chop. After all, the workers fed him such delicious snacks.

“Litter can make animals sick,” said Mr. Rivers, “or cause a forest fire.”

“But where’s the food?” whined B.B.

Mr. Rivers tapped his bag. “In here. You know our rule. Humans should never feed wild animals, and wild animals should never eat human food.”

Sheldon added, “You shouldn’t eat their food, and they shouldn’t cut down so many trees.”

“The workers are only taking dead trees,” B.B. protested. “What’s the harm in that?”

"I'll tell you," chimed a new voice. "My name's Skylar, and I'm looking for a home. We bluebirds live in dead trees, but I can't find one."

"Maybe we can help,"
offered Kingston.

"You would do that?"
chirped the bluebird.

"We're the Nature Squad. We'll
find a dead tree in no time."

B.B. remembered the old trees he had shown the workers. *If Skylar finds those trees, he'll move in. The workers won't come back, and I'll never get any leftovers. I can't let that happen.*

That gave B.B. an idea. "I'll do it," he offered. "I'll find that bluebird a house."

"A fine plan," Kingston declared.

The bear smiled. "I know just the place."

He led Skylar toward Baker's Pond. "This is it," said B.B., pointing toward a tall tree trunk.

"It's perfect!" the bluebird exclaimed.

"There's just one thing," noted B.B. "You'll be living with wood ducks."

“Come in,” said Woodra. “You’re welcome here.”

Skylar glided into his new home. The nest was lined with feathers, perfect for relaxing.

My search is over, thought the bluebird. He closed his eyes and slept.

The very next day, Woodra announced, “It’s time for you to go, dear.” She nudged him toward the hole.

“What do you mean?” asked Skylar.

“My ducklings jump out a day after hatching. You should too.” She nudged him again, harder this time.

Skylar tumbled out of the tree, landing with a thud.

“Sorry dear,” called Woodra. “I thought you could fly.”

“I can,” the bluebird pouted. “I’m not used to being pushed!”

He flapped his wings and soared skyward. He needed to find B.B.

"No problem," said the bear. "I have a backup plan."

He escorted his friend to a tree in the valley. "There's a beautiful nest up there. Some blue jays offered to share it."

Skylar fluttered to the nest.

"Make yourself at home," said Papa Jay.

Skylar nestled into a soft corner and closed his eyes. He could get used to living under the open sky.

Jay! Jay! Jay!

Skylar's eyes shot open. He pressed his wings against his ears. "What is that terrible noise?"

"Jay! Jay! Jay!" his nest mates sang. "What noise?"

"Do you shout like that a lot?" the bluebird asked.

"All day," replied Papa Jay.

Skylar sighed. "I can't live here." He thanked the blue jays and flew back to B.B.

"Don't worry," offered the bear. "I have one more idea."

He brought Skylar to see his turtle friend. “You can live in Sheldon’s shell,” B.B. declared.

The bluebird peeked inside. “I can’t do it,” he yelled. “It smells like lily pads in there!”

“And it’s kind of crowded,” added Sheldon.

Skylar dropped onto the grass.
"I'll never find a home," he cried.

A rumble filled the air.

"And now it's going to rain!"

B.B. knew it wouldn't rain. He was hungry again. *Is eating human food more important than finding Skylar a nest?* he wondered.

"I'll have to try a different forest," whimpered the bluebird.

"No," B.B. decided. "Come with me."

He gathered the Nature Squad and led Skylar to a gray corner of the woods.

“I was saving these trees for the workers,” said the bear. “You can live here instead.”

Skylar chirped excitedly. “Thank you, B.B. It’s a dream come true!”

“What about the humans?” asked Red. “Won’t they take these trees?”

"I'll tell them they've cut enough," said B.B. "If they chop down all the dead trees, the bluebirds, raccoons and other animals won't have a place to live."

"I'll come too," Mr. Rivers volunteered. "Someone should tell them not to feed the bears."

"So much damage has already been done," noted Skylar. "Is there anything we can do?"

Mr. Rivers smiled hopefully. "In fact, there is."

He showed the animals how to build nest boxes—little homes for birds. Then together, they spent the week making their forest a better place.

How to Build a Nest Box*

Materials needed:

untreated, weather-resistant wood (such as cedar):

1" x 6" x 4' board

1" x 10" x 10½" board (the roof)

20–25 nails, 2 screws, 1 double-headed nail

tools: saw, ruler, pencil, hammer, drill, chisel

Building instructions:

1. Divide the 1" x 6" x 4' board into pieces, as shown below.

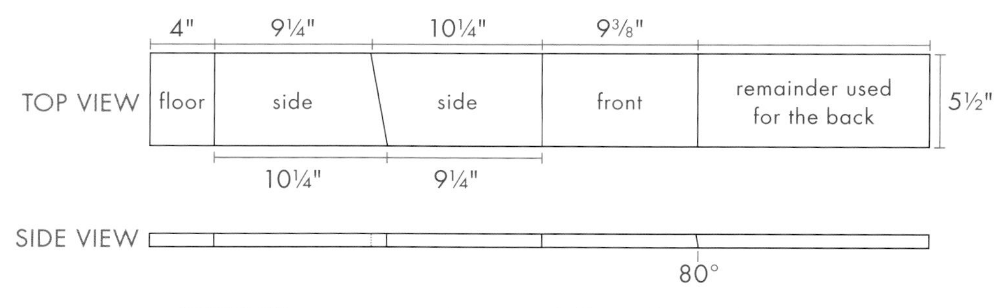

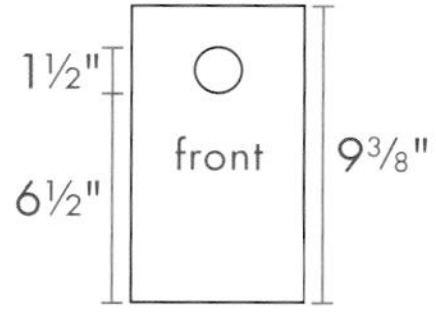

2. With your drill and chisel, create a 1½" hole on the front board. Center the hole between the side edges, about 6½" from the bottom.

3. Cut the corners off the floor piece, about ¼" from the tips, to allow for drainage.

* These instructions are intended for grown-ups.

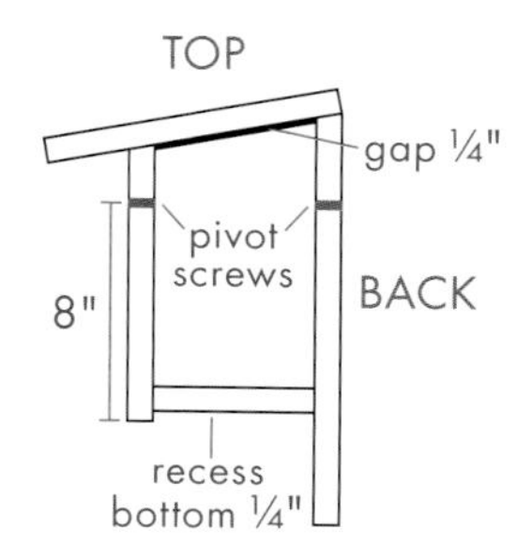

4. Nail together the front, back, bottom, roof and left side. The top piece should be flush with the back of the nest box and centered over the side edges. Take special care to leave a ¼" gap between the roof and each side piece. This will allow for ventilation.

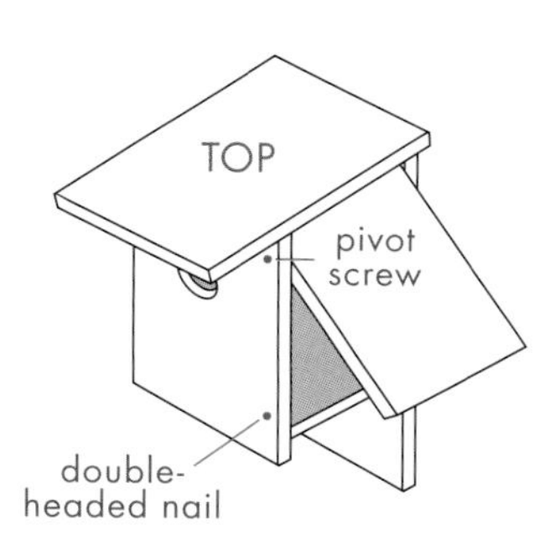

5. Put the right side into place and screw pivot points through the front and back pieces (into the side piece), about eight inches above the floor. This should hold the right side into place, while allowing you to easily flip it open as needed.

6. Drill a hole through the front piece (into the side piece) about two inches above the floor. Slide a double-headed nail into the hole to hold the door closed.

Mounting instructions:

1. Choose an open area within 100' of trees and well away from any buildings.

2. Mount the nest box 4–6' above ground, preferably on a post or pole facing a nearby tree or shrub. Some experts suggest facing the nest box east or north.

3. To keep predators away, create a funnel-shaped metal (such as tin) barrier and place it around the mounting surface, approximately 8" below the nest box.

Building a Better World:
Conservation Tips for Kids

1. RECYCLE

Set up three large containers in your home or classroom. Throw away plastic bottles in one, aluminum cans in another and paper (including newspapers) in the third. When the containers are full, ask a grown-up to help you recycle them.

2. PICK UP LITTER

Find and throw away at least three pieces of litter every day. But never grab anything sharp or pointy. Ask a grown-up for help with broken glass and litter that might cause a cut.

3. SAVE WATER

Turn off the faucet as you brush your teeth. Turn on the water only when it's time to rinse.

4. SHUT OFF LIGHTS

When you leave a room, turn off the lights (unless you are coming right back). Also shut off computers, TVs and video games when you are finished with them.

5. KEEP THE REFRIGERATOR DOOR CLOSED

Open the refrigerator only when you know what you need. Grab the item and quickly close the door again.

Did You Know?

BLACK BEARS

Don't let the name fool you. Black bears can be black or brown. I love to eat, but black bears are also known for how much we sleep. Every year, just before winter, I crawl into a cave or an underground hole, and I hibernate until spring. For six months, I don't eat or go to the bathroom. In fact, I spend most of that time sound asleep!

EASTERN BLUEBIRDS

I'm an eastern bluebird, one of three different types of bluebirds. The other two are western bluebirds and mountain bluebirds. I was nearly eliminated from many parts of the country—too many dead trees were chopped down, and I couldn't find a place to live. Thanks to all of the people who put up nest boxes, I'm back and better than ever!

WOOD DUCKS

Just like Skylar and his bluebird friends, we wood ducks live in old trees. Nest boxes are built for us too, so we have places to live. It's true what I said. A day after hatching, my chicks jump out of the nest. After that, they never return to the nest again.

BLUE JAYS

As far as birds go, we blue jays are some of the loudest. It's a good thing, too, because we have plenty of enemies (like cats and owls). I make loud noises to scare other animals away. I can even sound like a hawk, an owl or a cat. "Meow!" Pretty cool, huh?

About the Creators

Ryan Jacobson prides himself on writing stories with a positive message for children. Since he first began writing in 2005, Ryan has delved into such topics as self-confidence, choosing good role models and the positive power of imagination. Now, it is his honor to share a tale that puts the ability to "build a better world" into the hands of children. Ryan is the author of 14 books, including his first picture book, *Joe Lee and Boo*, and a choose your path book, *Lost in the Wild*. He lives in Mora, Minnesota, with his wife Lora, adopted sons Jonah and Lucas and their dog Boo. For more information about the author or to read his blog, visit www.RyanJacobsonOnline.com.

Raised in Burbank, California, Joel Seibel started his career in animation with Disney Studios at age 19. Four years later he moved to Hanna-Barbera Studios, where he spent 28 years working on such shows as *The Smurfs*, *Scooby-Doo* and about 200 other TV series. In 1994 he began working for Warner Brothers Studio as a storyboard artist on *Pinky and the Brain*, *Animaniacs* and *The Sylvester and Tweety Mysteries*. In 1996 Joel received a Primetime Emmy Award for designing *A Pinky and the Brain Christmas Special*. Next he joined Nickelodeon to storyboard *The Angry Beavers*. From 2007 to present Joel has storyboarded *My Little Pony*, *Care Bears* and *Angelina Ballerina*. Joel lives in northeastern Minnesota with his wife, Ellen.

The Forest Where Ashley Lives

This project was supported
in part, by a grant through the Iowa
Department of Natural Resources and from the
Urban Forestry Center for the Midwestern States of the
Northeastern Area State and Private Forestry, USDA Forest Service.

Illustrated by:
John L. Smith, Research Associate, Department of Forestry, Iowa State University, Ames, Iowa

Written by:
Mark A. Vitosh, Program Assistant, ISU Extension Forestry, and
Ashley L. Vitosh, 4th Grader, Crawford Elementary School, Ames, Iowa

Designed by:
Juls Design, Ankeny, Iowa

Edited by:
Elaine Edwards and Diane Nelson, Communication Specialists, ISU Extension

Published by:
Iowa State University Extension, Ames, Iowa

Thanks to all of the students and educators who assisted in evaluating the book.

ISBN 0-9700528-0-4

Library of Congress Cataloging-in-Publication Data
Vitosh, Mark A. (Mark Allen), 1966-
The forest where Ashley lives / written by Mark A. Vitosh; illustrated by John L. Smith.
p. cm.
Summary: A girl describes the variety of trees found in her town and how forests provide many benefits for people and animals.
ISBN 0-9700528-0-4 (paperback)
1. Trees in cities--Juvenile literature. [1. Trees in cities. 2. Trees.] I. Smith, John L. (John Lyle), 1964- ill. II. Title.

SB436 . V58 2000
635.9'77--dc21

00-039697

The Forest Where Ashley Lives

Written by Mark A. Vitosh and Ashley L. Vitosh
Illustrated by John L. Smith

Hi! My name is Ashley. I'm seven years old. I like to play soccer in the spring, ride my bike in the summer, make leaf piles in the fall, and build snowpeople in the winter. I also like to take walks around town with my dad and my dog, Ubu.

My dad is a tree person. He's called the "town forester" because he takes care of the trees in our town forest. Do you have a forest where you live?

Trees are everywhere in our town forest. They're in the park, at my school, near the creek and river, along the streets, and in people's yards.

Our town forest includes more than just a lot of trees. It also has people, buildings, houses, streets, cars, buses, and trucks.

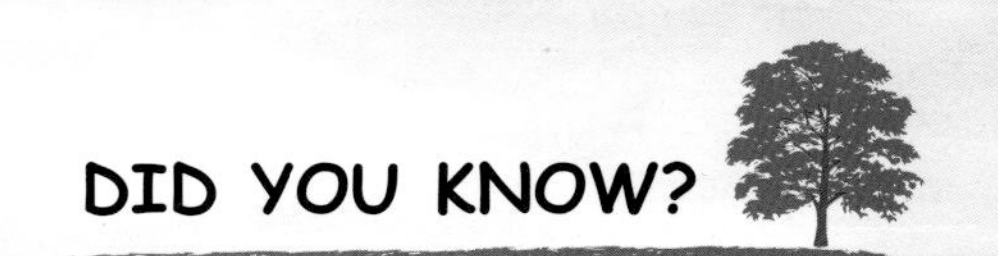

DID YOU KNOW?

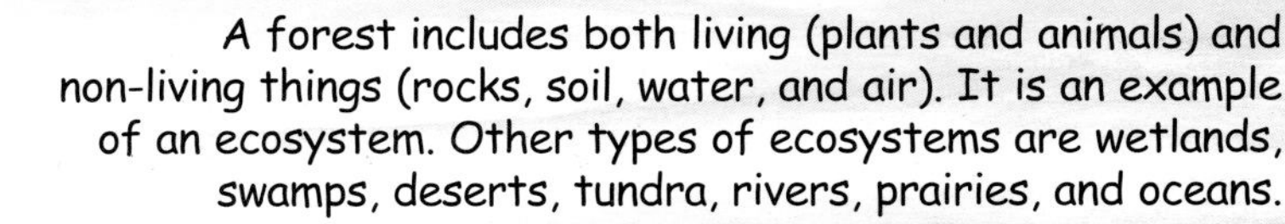

A forest includes both living (plants and animals) and non-living things (rocks, soil, water, and air). It is an example of an ecosystem. Other types of ecosystems are wetlands, swamps, deserts, tundra, rivers, prairies, and oceans.

Our town forest also has shrubs, flowers, vines, water, soil, animals, and mushrooms. If you live in a town or city, you probably live in a forest, too.

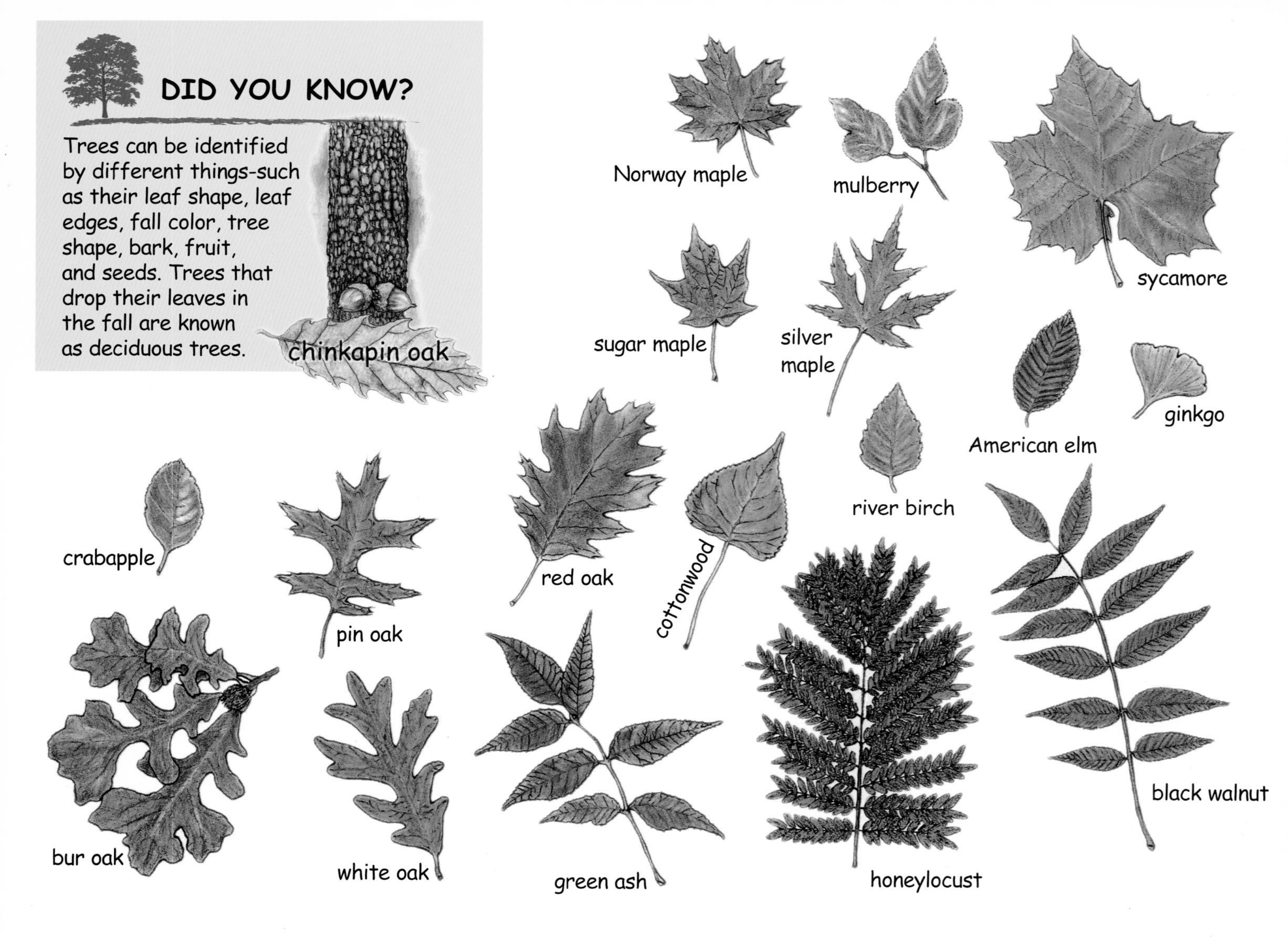

Many kinds of trees live in our town forest. Some have big broad leaves and names like maple, oak, ash, elm, and walnut. These trees lose their leaves in the fall.

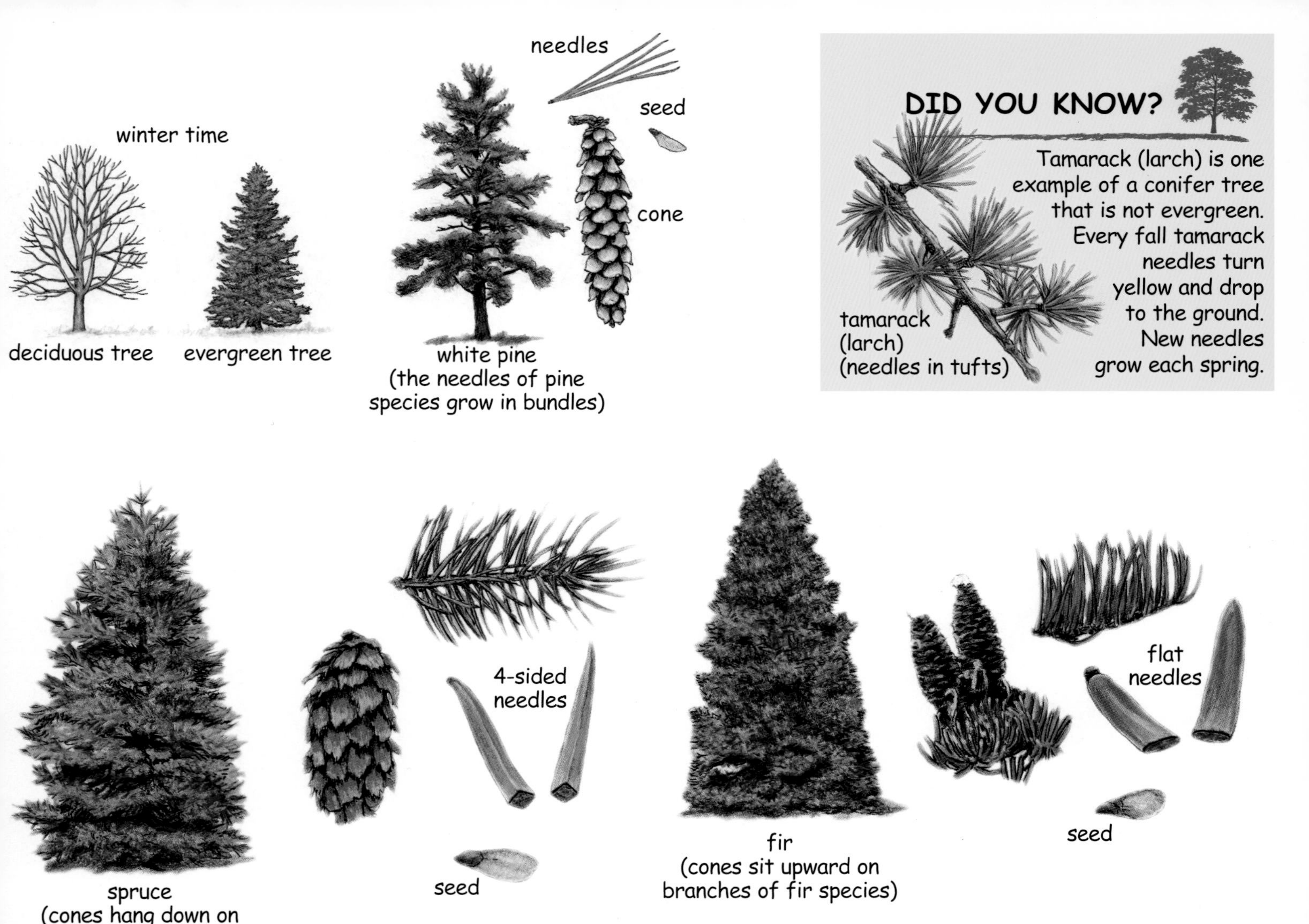

Conifer trees have thin needle-like leaves with names like pine, spruce, and fir. Most conifers stay green all year long, even in the winter. These trees are called "evergreen." All conifers make cones that hold seeds. What kinds of trees are in your forest?

Our town forest has many different sizes of trees. Some are tall, some are short, and some are in between. Just like people, the trees are all different ages. My dad told me that the biggest trees are not always the oldest. Some trees can grow more than 4 feet a year, while others may only grow 6 to 24 inches in a year.

Forests provide many benefits for people and animals. My dad told me that trees and other plants release the invisible gas called oxygen that is needed by all living things to survive. Wow! This means trees and other plants help us stay alive!

Trees are like big air conditioners that run all summer long. My sister, Abbey, and I like to play in the shade of our big trees. It would be really hot in the summer without any trees!

Some trees are helpful in the wintertime, too. The pine trees in our backyard stay green all year long. They act like a wall to keep winter winds from blowing against our house. They protect the rabbits in my backyard, too, by giving them a sheltered place to live.

Our forest provides a home for animals such as squirrels, birds, rabbits, owls, raccoons, butterflies, and beetles. Trees also provide food for some animals.

The trees, shrubs, and grasses in our forest help the water we drink at home and school stay clean. Tree and other plant roots filter out some unwanted materials in the water as it moves through the ground. Roots also help hold the soil so it doesn't wash away when it rains or when the snow melts. Without the help of tree and other plant roots, the water could get really yucky!

Trees provide many benefits. They help cool the air, clean the water, provide homes and food for animals, and provide oxygen for us to breathe. They also make our town look pretty! In order to do all these things trees and forests have to be healthy. Foresters like my dad help trees grow strong and healthy.

One day, I went to work with my dad. At first I was mad because his workers cut down some trees. But then my dad told me that sometimes sick or injured trees have to be removed so they won't fall on houses or people.

The best way to help the forest every time a tree is cut down is to plant new trees to replace it. Every spring we have a special tree planting day called Arbor Day. My dad lets me help.

When I was four years old, my dad and I planted a tree for Arbor Day. We went to a tree farm, which is called a nursery, to choose the tree. We picked a white ash. It was neat, because this tree had the same name as me. My dad calls it Ashley's tree.

The first thing we did when we planted my tree was to dig a big wide hole. Then we put the tree in the middle of the hole, and then we put the same soil back into the hole to cover up the roots. Next we covered the ground around the tree with wood chips. Finally we gave the tree plenty of water.

To protect my tree, Dad told me not to break the branches, hit it with a lawnmower or weed-whipper, carve my name on it, or tie my dog Ubu to it. Instead, I water the tree when it is hot and dry, and my dad helps the tree become stronger by cutting and removing broken and weak branches. He does this to all of the trees in town at different times to help them stay healthy and strong.

Trees are neat living things, and we really need them in our towns and cities. They will always help us, if we help them. Now that you know so much about trees and forests, you can enjoy the ones where you live!